TO
ANNIE

JACK KENT'S
MERRY
MOTHER
GOOSE

Pictures By Jack Kent

To - Sean
From - Bonnie +
Kevin Greenwood

gb Golden Press • New York
Western Publishing Company, Inc.
Racine, Wisconsin

Sing a song of sixpence,
A pocket full of rye;
Four-and-twenty blackbirds
Baked in a pie.

When the pie was opened,
The birds began to sing;

Wasn't that a dainty dish
To set before the king?

Old King Cole was a merry old soul,
And a merry old soul was he;

He called for his pipe,

And he called for his bowl,

And he called for his fiddlers three.

There was an old woman
called Nothing-at-all,
Who lived in a dwelling
exceedingly small.

A man stretched his mouth
to its utmost extent,

And down at one gulp
house and old woman went.

To market, to market,
to buy a fat pig,

Home again, home again,
jiggety-jig;

To market, to market,
to buy a fat hog,
Home again, home again,
jiggety-jog.

Little Jack Horner
Sat in a corner,
Eating a Christmas pie.

He put in his thumb,

And pulled out a plum,

And said, "What a good boy am I!"

Jerry Hall, he is so small,

A rat could eat him,
hat and all.

PTUI

Polly put the kettle on,
Polly put the kettle on,
Polly put the kettle on,
We'll all have tea.

Sukey take it off again,
Sukey take it off again,

Sukey take it off again,
They've all gone away.

Little Robin Redbreast

came to visit me.

This is what he whistled:

"Thank you for my tea."

As I was going to Bonner,

BONNER

I met a pig

WITHOUT A WIG!

Upon my word
of honor!

12

As I was going to St. Ives,
I met a man with seven wives.
Each wife had seven sacks,
Each sack had seven cats,
Each cat had seven kits.

Kits, cats, sacks, and wives,
How many were going to St. Ives?

(One—only I was going to St. Ives.)

13

Dame Trot and her cat
Sat down for a chat.
The Dame sat on this side
And Puss sat on that.

"Puss," says the Dame,
"Can you catch a rat?"

"Or a mouse in
the dark?"

"Purr," says the cat.

"Pussycat, Pussycat,
 where have you been?"
"I've been to London
 to look at the queen."

"Pussycat, Pussycat,
 what did you there?"

"I frightened a little mouse
 under the chair."

Alas! Alas! for Miss Mackay!

Her knives and forks have run away!

And when her cups and spoons are going,
She's sure she has no way of knowing.

Old Mother Hubbard
Went to the cupboard,
To get her poor dog
    a bone;

But when she got there,

The cupboard was bare,

And so the poor dog had none.

17

Doctor Foster went to Gloucester in a shower of rain.

He stepped in a puddle
Right up to his middle,

And never went there again.

There was an old woman who lived in a shoe.
She had so many children she didn't know what to do.
She gave them some broth, without any bread,
And whipped them all soundly and sent them to bed.

Three wise men of Gotham,

They went to sea in a bowl.

If the bowl had been stronger,

My song had been longer.

Rub-a-dub-dub, three men in a tub,   And who do you think they be?

The butcher, the baker, the candlestick maker. Turn 'em out, knaves all three!

There was once a fish. (What more could you wish?)

He lived in the sea. (Where else would he be?)

He was caught on a line. (Whose line if not mine?)

So I brought him to you. (What else should I do?)

There was an old man
And he had a calf,

And that's half.

He took him out of the stall,

And put him on the wall,

And that's all.

"Bow-wow," says the dog,
"Meow, meow," says the cat,
"Grunt, grunt," goes the hog,
And "Squeak," goes the rat.
"Tu-whu," says the owl,
"Caw, caw," says the crow,
"Quack, quack," says the duck,
And what cuckoos say you know.

Wouldn't it be funny . . .
    Wouldn't it now . . .
If the dog said, "Moo-oo"
    And the cow said, "Bow-wow?"
If the cat sang and whistled,
    And the bird said, "Meow?"
Wouldn't it be funny . . .
    Wouldn't it now?

Anna Maria, she sat on the fire,

The fire was too hot, she sat on the pot,

The pot was too round, she sat on the ground,

The ground was too flat, she sat on the cat,

The cat ran away with Maria on her back.

Pussycat ate the dumplings,

Pussycat ate the dumplings!

Mama stood by and cried,

OH, FIE!
WHY DID YOU EAT
THE DUMPLINGS?

Ply the spade and ply the hoe.
Plant the seed,

And it will grow.

25

Ding, dong, bell,
Pussy's in the well.

Who put her in?
Little Johnny Green.

Who pulled her out?
Little Tommy Stout.

What a naughty boy was that,
To try to drown poor pussycat,

Who never did any harm,
And killed the mice in his father's barn.

Jack and Jill went up the hill

To fetch a pail of water.

Jack fell down

And broke his crown

And Jill came tumbling after.

Once I saw a little bird come hop,

hop,

hop.

And I cried:

Little bird, will you stop,

STOP,

STOP?

28

The cat sat asleep
by the side of the fire,
The mistress snored
loud as a pig.

Jack took up his fiddle
by Jenny's desire,

And struck up a bit of a jig.

Jack Sprat
could eat no fat,
His wife
could eat no lean;

And so between them both, you see, they licked the platter clean.

Cock a doodle doo! My dame has lost her shoe.

My master's lost his fiddling stick,

GIMME!

And knows not what to do.

The Queen of Hearts
She made some tarts,
All on a summer's day.

The Knave of Hearts
He stole the tarts,
And took them clean away.

The King of Hearts called for the tarts,
And beat the Knave
full sore.

The Knave of Hearts brought back the tarts,
And vowed he'd steal no more.

The lion and the unicorn

were fighting for the crown;

The lion beat the unicorn all about the town.

The man in brown
Soon brought him down.

Dickory, dickory,
dare,
The pig flew up
in the air;

Dickory, dickory, dare.

There was an old woman
　　tossed up in a basket,
Seventeen times
　　as high as the moon;
And where she was going
　　I couldn't but ask it,
For under her arm
　　She carried a broom.
"Old woman, old woman,
　　old woman," quoth I,
"Whither, O whither, O whither so high?"
"To sweep the cobwebs out of the sky!
And I'll be with you by and by."

The Man in the Moon looked out of the moon,
And this is what he said,
" 'Tis time that, now I'm getting up,
All wee ones were in bed."

"What's the news of the day,
Good neighbor, I pray?"
"They say a balloon
Is gone up to the moon!"

Wear you a hat
　　or wear you a crown,
All that goes up
　　must surely come down.

There was an old woman
　　who rode on a broom,
With a high gee ho, gee humble;
And she took her old cat
　　behind for a groom,
With a bimble, bamble, bumble.

Old Mother Goose, when
　　she wanted to wander,
Would ride through the air
　　on a very fine gander.

"Flying-man, Flying-man, up in the sky,
Where are you going to, flying so high?"
"Over the mountains and over the sea!"
"Flying-man, Flying-man, can't you take me?"

35

Little Miss Muffet
Sat on a tuffet,
Eating of curds and whey.

There came a great spider,
Who sat down beside her,

And frightened Miss Muffet away.

Baby and I

were baked

in a pie.

The gravy was wonderful hot!

We had nothing to pay to the baker that day
And so we crept out of the pot.

There was an old woman of Harrow,
Who visited in a wheelbarrow,

And her servant before
Knocked loud at each door,

To announce the old woman of Harrow.

Jack be nimble,

Jack be quick,

Jack jump over the candlestick.

What did I dream?
I do not know;

The fragments fly
like chaff.

Yet strange my mind
was tickled so,

I cannot help but laugh.

Hickety, pickety, my black hen,

She lays eggs
for gentlemen.

Gentlemen come every day
To see what my black hen doth lay.

I had a little dog, and his name was Blue Bell.

I gave him some work,

And he did it very well.

This little piggie went to market,

This little piggie stayed home,

This little piggie had roast beef,

This little piggie had none,

And this little piggie cried, "Wee, wee, wee!" all the way home.

Hannah Bantry,
In the pantry,

Gnawing at
a mutton bone.

How she gnawed it, how she clawed it,
When she found herself alone.

Ask your mother for fifty cents
To see the elephant jump the fence.

He jumped so high

He touched the sky,

And never came down 'til the Fourth of July.

Hey, diddle, diddle!
The cat
and the
fiddle,

The cow
jumped
over
the moon.

The little
dog laughed
to see
such sport,

And the
dish ran
away with
the spoon.

Little Bo-peep
Has lost her sheep,

And can't tell where
to find them.

Leave them alone,
And they'll come home,
And bring their tails
behind them.

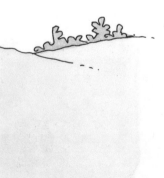

Mary had a little lamb, its fleece was white as snow,

And everywhere that Mary went, the lamb was sure to go.

Index of First Lines